D0046180

Martin Bridge
Ready for Takeoff!

Written by
Jessica Scott
Kerrin

Illustrated by
Joseph Kelly

Kids Can Press

For Peter and Elliott Kerrin,
with special thanks to Jane Buss,
Trudy Carey, Debbie Rogosin
and Noreen Smiley — J.S.K.

For backbone, from wishbone — Kel

Text © 2005 Jessica Scott Kerrin
Illustrations © 2005 Joseph Kelly

Kids Can Press gratefully acknowledges the financial support of the Government of Ontario, through the Ontario Media Development Corporation; the Ontario Arts Council; the Canada Council for the Arts; and the Government of Canada, through the CBF, for our publishing activity.

Published in Canada and the U.S. by Kids Can Press Ltd.
25 Dockside Drive, Toronto, ON M5A 0B5

Kids Can Press is a Corus Entertainment Inc. company

www.kidscanpress.com

Edited by Debbie Rogosin
Designed by Julia Naimska

The art in this book was drawn with graphite and charcoal; shading was added digitally.
The text is set in GarthGraphic.

Printed and bound in Shenzen, China, in 7/2018 by C&C Offset

CM 05 0 9 8 7 6 5 4
CM PA 05 20 19 18 17 16 15 14 13 12 11

Library and Archives Canada Cataloguing in Publication

Kerrin, Jessica Scott
        Martin Bridge ready for takeoff! / written by Jessica Scott Kerrin ; illustrated by Joseph Kelly.

ISBN 978-1-55337-688-0 (bound)
ISBN 978-1-55337-772-6 (pbk.)

I. Kelly, Joseph II. Title.

PS8621.E77M37 2005   jC813'.6   C2004-903282-8

Contents

Riddles

Martin held his breath as he slowly poured Zip Rideout Space Flakes into his official Zip-approved cosmic cereal bowl. Maybe this will be the morning a prize falls out! Zip promised one in every box. Martin's bowl started to overflow, but no prize today.

Oh well. Martin added milk and began to munch on the sugary star and comet shapes. He turned the cereal box around so he could look at his hero while he ate.

Martin was three-quarters of the way through his breakfast when his dad came into the kitchen.

"Better get a move on, Sport."

Martin looked up at the wall clock with a jolt. Cripes.

He whipped open the hall closet and yanked his raincoat off the hanger. He tugged on his rubber boots and stood up.

Cripes. Wrong feet.

He pulled them off and tried again.

"Mrs. Phips is going to kill me," he muttered to himself. Mrs. Phips was his cranky-pants bus driver. Martin had had her since first grade. He often complained about her, but his mom and dad always said the same thing.

"So, don't keep her waiting then."

Martin grabbed his knapsack and charged out the front door.

"Make the bus late. Make the bus late," Martin chanted to himself. Raindrops dimpled the puddles as he splashed down the driveway. When he rounded the corner,

the grumble of the waiting bus drowned out the swish, swish, swish of his raincoat.

Cripes. Mrs. Phips was sure to yell at him for being late again.

The bus door folded open with a whoosh. Martin took a deep breath and scrambled on board.

Only it wasn't Mrs. Phips.

"Hi there. I'm Jenny."

Martin couldn't believe his luck. He looked around. As usual, his best friend Stuart sat at the back along with the rest of the passengers.

"Where's Mrs. Phips?" Martin asked.

"She's in the hospital. Hurt her hip. I'll be your driver until she gets better," said Jenny. "So, what's your name?"

"Martin," he said.

"Martin," repeated Jenny thoughtfully. She pulled the lever to close the door, then smiled at his reflection in the rearview mirror.

"Say, Martin, do you like riddles?"

"Sure," said Martin. He shrugged at Stuart and then sat across from Jenny. Truth was, he loved riddles. The bus lurched forward, and the windshield wipers flapped against the rain.

"Okay then. What do clouds carry after they stop raining?"

"I don't know," said Martin. "What do clouds carry after they stop raining?"

"A sunbrella," said Jenny. "They carry a sunbrella."

Martin laughed.

"So how come everyone's sitting at the back?" asked Jenny.

Martin knew that the passengers sat as far away from Mrs. Phips as possible.

"They probably didn't know you had a riddle," he said. Jenny nodded.

"What was so funny?" Stuart asked when they got off the bus at school.

Martin told him the riddle.

"Good one," said Stuart.

"What's good?" asked Alex, Martin's

other best friend. He lived too close to take
the bus, but he always met them at the front
door of the school. Even on rainy days.

"We have a new driver," said Martin.

"Where's Mrs. Phips?"

"Hospital," said Martin. "I don't know for how long." He told Alex the riddle as they splashed their way up the steps to the school.

"I don't get it," said Alex.

Stuart rolled his eyes. Martin explained it, and Alex laughed, too.

Martin told the joke all day to anyone who would listen, and he was first on board for the ride home.

"My friends liked your riddle," he told Jenny, water dripping from his raincoat to a puddle at his feet.

"I'm glad," said Jenny. "How was your day?"

Martin had planned to sit at the back, but now he paused. *How was his day?* The only thing Mrs. Phips ever asked was if he'd forgotten to wear his watch.

So Martin sat across from Jenny. He told her about the Junior Badgers and how they were going to build model rockets. He told her about Ginny, his neighbor's pet hamster. He told her about Clark, who ate anything on a dare, and Laila, whose big curly hair blocked his view of the blackboard.

He talked about his two best friends, Stuart and Alex, and about how Alex had too many brothers and wanted his own room. He told her about his favorite cartoon, *Zip Rideout: Space Cadet,* which he watched every day after school. He even told her that one of his paintings had been selected for the display case at school that week.

Martin usually only bragged to his mom, but somehow this last tidbit just popped out. Jenny whistled at his good news. Martin shrugged modestly.

"Here's your stop," said Jenny as she pulled over at Martin's driveway. Martin looked around, surprised. Rides with Mrs. Phips always took forever.

"I'll have a new riddle for you tomorrow," said Jenny as Martin jumped off.

She waved good-bye and closed the door.

Mrs. Phips never told riddles, thought Martin. He waved until the bus disappeared. Then he noticed something else. It had finally stopped raining.

The next morning, Martin gathered his things.

Knapsack?

Check.

Lunch bag?

Check.

"Good-bye!" he called and headed out the door in plenty of time. He stood at the top of the driveway and watched as headlights rounded the corner. It was Jenny.

"Good morning, Martin," said Jenny.

Well! Mrs. Phips never remembered anyone's name. Mostly she'd yell, "You kids!"

as in "You kids better keep it down back there!"

Martin waved to Stuart and sat across from Jenny again.

"What smells so nice?" he asked.

"A little air freshener," said Jenny. "It's supposed to smell like a spring meadow."

Mrs. Phips always smelled like old bus seats.

"Ready for today's riddle?"

Martin nodded.

"What did the jealous rain cloud say when the sun burst through?"

"What?" asked Martin.

"You stole my thunder!" said Jenny.

Martin laughed. So did a few passengers who had moved closer to the front to listen.

Jenny's purple jacket shimmered in the

sun as she turned the wheel. Mrs. Phips always wore gray. Martin wasn't sure if gray was even a color.

That afternoon in art class, Alex visited Martin at his easel. They had been told to paint a spring scene. Martin had decided to

paint a meadow of flowers in his new favorite color.

"Holy cow!" said Alex. "That's a lot of purple!"

Martin nodded and stood back to admire his work. This was his best painting ever.

Each day Jenny offered a new riddle. More and more passengers tried to guess the answer, and one by one they moved to the front with Jenny. Her laughter filled the bus.

"Jenny is the best driver in the world," wrote Martin in thick red pencil in his notebook. And it wasn't just the riddles. She played Eye Spy games, led sing-alongs and told terrific stories about backpacking around the world. Her bus always arrived at school before the bell. No one ever kept Jenny waiting.

"I want to do something nice for Jenny," Martin told his mom when he got home from school one day.

"I'm glad you like her," said his mom. "I wonder how Mrs. Phips is doing."

Martin stiffened. He hadn't thought of Mrs. Phips in ages. "Mrs. Phips doesn't tell riddles," he said dully.

"I know," said his mom, "but she'll be out of the hospital soon. Perhaps you could do something nice for her, too."

Martin almost laughed out loud at that crazy suggestion, but his mom crossed her arms.

"Zip's on," mumbled Martin, and he turned to the television.

Later Martin went upstairs to think. As he brushed his teeth, a wonderful idea

came to him. He spit the toothpaste out and called Stuart.

"Let's decorate Jenny's bus!" suggested Martin.

"How?" Stuart asked.

"With tissue paper flowers," said Martin. "Like the ones you see on floats in parades. If everyone makes a few and tapes them on, Jenny's bus will be covered."

"Great idea," said Stuart. "My mom's got leftover tissue paper from the last store window she decorated."

"Perfect!" said Martin. "We can hand out the paper tomorrow."

At morning recess, Martin and Stuart handed out tissue paper to Jenny's passengers.

"Remember," explained Martin. "Stick

your flowers on the bus tomorrow morning."

"Just before you get on!" added Stuart.

"That way it will be a surprise!"
finished Martin.

The schoolyard buzzed with excitement.

At home that night, Martin made the best decoration of all. He painted a sign that read "World's Best Driver." The letters were huge. And purple.

After a hasty breakfast, Martin rolled up the sign and tucked it under his arm. He bounded to the top of his driveway and looked for Stuart.

Stuart was supposed to get up extra early and walk to Martin's stop. But he wasn't there. Martin passed the rolled-up sign from one sweaty hand to the other.

There! Stuart rounded the corner and ran full-out toward him. "Sign?" was all Stuart could ask as he gasped for breath.

"Got it," said Martin. "You had me worried. Look!"

The bus rumbled into view. Its side was covered with a colorful bouquet.

"Wow!" said Stuart, still puffing.

"Remember the plan," said Martin. His heart pounded.

Whoosh! The bus door folded open. Stuart slapped on two flowers, one from each pocket. Then he bent down and pretended to tie his shoe right in front of the door. This gave Martin the time he needed to secretly tape his sign to the side of the bus.

"Done!" whispered Martin.

Stuart nodded and stood up. They grinned at each other before Stuart bounded up the steps. Martin followed right behind but bumped into Stuart, who had stopped short. Confused, Martin took a step back. As he looked down the aisle, his smile faded.

Rows and rows of faces stared straight ahead. Everyone was crowded at the back, just like the old days. Nobody spoke. Stuart bolted to join them, leaving Martin alone with the driver.

Mrs. Phips was back.

"Shake a leg," growled Mrs. Phips, "or we'll be late."

Martin stumbled past the staring faces. He plunked down beside Stuart. Thick silence filled the bus all the way to school, except for the one word Stuart whispered to Martin.

"Ka-boom," he said, throwing up his arms. Stuart said "ka-boom" whenever something went wrong.

When they got off the bus, everyone pressed together in a huddle and watched Mrs. Phips park. They all spoke at once.

"Are we in trouble, Martin?"

"This was all your idea!"

"Do you think Mrs. Phips will notice the decorations?"

"Quick! Let's go before she sees us."

And they scrambled up the steps, disappearing inside.

Martin slid behind his desk. He opened his notebook and read "Jenny is the best driver in the world." Martin closed the book and sank further into his seat. His
stomach felt like it was filled with rocks.

"Today, class, I want you to paint something you see every day on the way home from school," suggested the art teacher.

Martin set up his easel. He dabbed his brush into all sorts of colors, but he couldn't stop worrying about Mrs. Phips.

"What happened?" asked Alex near the end of class. He stared at Martin's picture.

Martin shook his head. He had mixed too many paints, and now everything was dull gray. His sky was gray. His tree-lined street was gray. Even the school bus pulling up to his driveway was gray, gray, gray.

Martin sighed. He put his paints away without a word. For the rest of the day, Martin's mood stayed the same color as the drive-home picture he had crumpled into a ball.

It was easy to pick out Mrs. Phips's bus from the plain yellow ones lined up for the ride home. It still wore a million colorful flowers and had "World's Best Driver" plastered on its side.

Martin pulled his shoulders to his ears and climbed on board. He was heading straight to the back when he heard his name.

"Hello, Martin," said Mrs. Phips.

Startled, Martin looked around, saucer-eyed.

"You … you know my name?"

"I do now. Everyone's been talking about you."

"Oh," said Martin in a little voice. He saw Stuart waving frantically for Martin to join him at the back.

"Thanks for the flowers," continued Mrs. Phips. There was less gravel in her voice than usual. "And the sign." Her eyes softened. "I never knew you kids felt that way."

Cripes.

Martin's ears burned. His feet began to sweat in his runners. He turned to leave.

"When Jenny came by with the bus keys, she told me you liked riddles," said Mrs. Phips.

Martin turned back slowly. "Do ... do you know any?"

"No," said Mrs. Phips. "But Jenny gave me this." She reached down beside her seat and pulled out a book of riddles. Martin remembered Jenny's first riddle. He smiled.

"I have one," said Martin. "What do clouds carry after they stop raining?"

"I don't know, Martin. What *do* clouds carry after they stop raining?"

He told her.

"Good one!" said Mrs. Phips. She laughed. Mrs. Phips actually laughed!

Martin shrugged at Stuart and sat across from Mrs. Phips. The bus rumbled out of the parking lot. Outside the rattling window, the view was the same. Inside, the smell of old bus seats filled the air.

Mrs. Phips was still dressed like a foggy meadow. But when car horns toot-tooted at the decorated bus, everyone cheered and whistled.

"Toot back, Mrs. Phips, toot back!"

And before Martin knew it, he was home.

Faster Blaster

"Better go feed Ginny," reminded Martin's mom. She always did her reminding right in the middle of a *Zip Rideout* show. Cripes.

Ginny was Alice's pet hamster, and Alice lived three driveways down. Martin was feeding Ginny while Alice's family was on vacation. But just then, Zip had crash-landed on an unknown planet. It was orange. Martin sighed.

"Are they coming back today?" he asked as Zip stepped out of his rocket and tested the air.

"Yes," said his mom. She set down a bucket of cleaning supplies and handed him their neighbor's house key. "When you

get back, I'll need you to go through your closet. See if there are some clothes that no longer fit or toys you don't play with anymore."

Zip pulled out his blaster.

"Say, have you seen my Zip Rideout H_2O Faster Blaster?" he asked. His Auntie Joan had bought it for him during her last visit.

"For goodness sake, Martin! No, for the hundredth time!"

His mom did not like toy guns, even harmless water pistols. Zip began to blast warning shots at a gigantic green-scaled monster that had charged him from behind a pile of orange boulders. The monster stopped and held up its claws in surrender, but Martin knew that Zip was suspicious.

He could tell by the way Zip narrowed his eyes as the monster slowly moved toward him.

None of that mattered to Martin's mom, who flicked off the television.

Martin groaned. She shot him her no-nonsense spring-cleaning look, grabbed her bucket and disappeared upstairs.

Martin knew better than to turn the television back on. He wandered into the kitchen where his dad sat at the table.

"Hi, Dad," he said.

"Hi, Sport."

"Mom's spring cleaning today," warned Martin.

"Uh-oh." Martin's dad looked up from the newspaper. They both knew it would be safer to tackle a gigantic green-scaled

monster than to get between her and their stuffed closets.

Martin jerked open the refrigerator door and pulled out some crisp lettuce.

"I'm going over to feed Ginny," he said as he headed out. He whistled to himself as

he counted the driveways and turned up the one to Alice's house. He unlocked the back door and paused. Strange. It was quiet. Usually he could hear the whir of Ginny's running wheel. She must still be asleep.

Martin continued to whistle as he walked down the hallway and into the family room. Phew! What an odd smell! Like gym lockers after soccer practice, only worse.

Inside the cage, Ginny lay on her back, dainty feet in the air.

"Morning, Ginny," called Martin.

He pulled out her food tray and tore the lettuce into hamster-sized bites.

"Rise and shine," he called, sounding like his dad. "Breakfast time, sleepyhead." Ginny didn't budge.

"Not hungry?" he asked. He took a closer look at Ginny. He blinked. She did not blink back. A bone-numbing chill grew from deep in Martin's stomach and spread all the way to the tips of his fingers and toes.

"Ginny?" he squeaked.

Ginny didn't answer.

Oh no! Martin backed away, then bolted for the door. When he got home, he tore from room to room until he found his mom upstairs scrubbing a cupboard in the bathroom.

"What is it, Martin?"

"I think Ginny's sick."

"Sick?"

"Really sick."

"Really sick? What do you mean?"

"You know." Martin leaned forward and whispered. "Dead."

"Dead?"

Martin straightened up. "I'm pretty sure."

Martin had seen dead things before.

Like flattened porcupines on the highway. Or squished jellyfish washed up at low tide. Or the robin that flew against their living room window last year. But never someone's pet.

"We'd better go see," said his mom as she snapped off her scrubbing gloves.

Martin followed her back to Alice's house. Together they peered inside Ginny's cage.

"She hasn't moved," whispered Martin. His knees wobbled.

His mom gently tapped the cage. Bells rang and the running wheel rattled, but Ginny still didn't budge. Martin turned away from her empty black eyes.

"Oh, dear," said his mom in a hushed voice.

"Should we call a vet?" asked Martin, even though he already knew the answer.

"I don't think so, Martin," said his mom.

Martin found it hard to swallow past the tight lump that rose in his throat.

"Did I do something wrong?" he forced out in a creaky voice.

"No! You took excellent care of Ginny," she said, giving him a firm hug. "Sometimes these things happen no matter what."

Martin nodded, but then he had another alarming thought.

"We'll have to tell Alice!" A fresh wave of guilt washed over him.

"Yes, little Alice," she said thoughtfully. "I'd better call her mom before they leave."

Martin took his mom's hand as they

walked back home. They went into the kitchen, and she looked up the telephone number where Alice's family was staying.

As she began to dial, Martin quietly left the room. He didn't want to hear any of their conversation, so he turned the

television back on. Zip's theme song
told him the show was over.

Martin heard the kitchen door shut. He
got up and went to the window. Outside, his

mom talked to his dad in the yard. His dad nodded, disappeared into the garage and then headed out the driveway with a shovel and a little box tucked under his arm.

Martin sat down again when he heard the kitchen door open. His mom joined him on the sofa and patted his knee.

"Alice's mom told me that Ginny was a very old hamster."

"Alice will still be sad," said Martin, shaking his head.

"Yes, about that," she said. "Alice's mom would like us to buy a new hamster before they get home."

"A new hamster?" repeated Martin. "But it won't be the same as Ginny."

"No," agreed his mom. "But they want it to *look* like Ginny."

"*Look* like Ginny?" repeated Martin. "Why's that?"

Martin's mom didn't say anything.

Martin gave her a long look. "Oh, I get it," he said at last. "They don't want Alice to find out that Ginny died."

"You're right," she said carefully. "They don't."

"But it's lying," said Martin gravely.

Martin's mom took his hand in hers. "Well ... perhaps we can think of it as fibbing."

"Same thing," said Martin. His words fell out like stones.

"I suppose they think Alice is too little to understand," his mom suggested.

Martin's jaw dropped.

"Too little?" he repeated. *"Too little?"*

Horrified, Martin pulled his hand away.
"I was little once. Did you ever lie to me?"
he demanded.

"Of course not. I'd never lie to you."

Just then, a Zip Rideout H_2O Faster
Blaster commercial came on. Martin
frowned. "What about my Faster Blaster?"

"I told you. I haven't seen it. But perhaps

it will show up while I'm spring cleaning."

Fat chance, thought Martin. She hated that Faster Blaster. Said so a hundred times. Now it had mysteriously disappeared. He narrowed his eyes like Zip Rideout.

Martin's dad came in and scooped up his wallet and keys from the hall table. "Come on, Sport!" he called. "We're off to the pet store."

Martin didn't budge.

"You two go," said his mom, ruffling Martin's hair. "I'll keep working." She went to kiss Martin, but he dodged her and ducked out the door.

"Dad?" asked Martin after they had driven in silence for a while. "Do you think we should be doing this?"

"What do you mean, Sport?"

"Buying a hamster. Not telling Alice."

"Well, I suppose Alice's mom thinks Alice is too young to understand."

"But it's not the truth."

"I'm sure her mom will tell Alice when she gets older."

"Really? How old?"

"Old enough to understand."

Martin mulled this over. He'd always

been told to tell the truth. Now his dad was
buying into this fibbing thing, too. Martin
slumped in his seat.

"Are you okay?" asked his dad when
they pulled into the parking lot.

"I guess," muttered Martin. But when
they walked into the pet store, Martin
followed his dad with squinty eyes all the
way to the hamster
section.

"That one,"
Martin announced
grumpily after
peering from
cage to cage. He
pointed to a
hamster spinning
on a wheel.

Martin's dad waved the store clerk over.

Once the purchase was made, the store clerk asked, "What will you name her?"

"Fake-o Ginny," said Martin bitterly.

"That's unusual," said the store clerk.

Martin's dad hurried Martin out the door. They got in the van and drove home with Fake-o Ginny in a box on Martin's lap. Martin's dad chatted  about this and that while Martin stared out the window. He was running through a list of all the things his parents might have fibbed to him about. Would broccoli really make him strong? Did soap really kill germs? Were there really no gigantic green-scaled monsters under his bed?

At that thought, Martin sat up. He wouldn't have to worry about monsters if he had his Faster Blaster handy.

"Have you seen my Zip Rideout H_2O Faster Blaster?"

"No," said his dad, keeping his eyes on the road.

Martin thought he had said "no" just a little too quickly. His dad did not like toy guns, either. Martin frowned out the window.

Back at Alice's house, Martin and his dad watched as Fake-o Ginny sniffed around the old Ginny's cage. Then she jumped onto the running wheel for a spin.

"Seems happy enough," said his dad.

"I suppose we should head home. See if your mom needs help."

Martin's mom came downstairs when she heard them arrive. Bags of old clothes and other assorted oddities were piled at the kitchen door.

"How'd it go?" she asked, looking anxiously from Martin to his dad.

"Good," said his dad.

Martin ignored the question. He eyed the bags. "Did you find my Zip Rideout H_2O Faster Blaster?" he demanded.

"No, Martin. Sorry."

"And you've cleaned absolutely everywhere?" he pressed.

"Try to think of the last place you had it," she suggested.

Whoa! thought Martin. She hadn't answered his question. Something was definitely up. Martin said nothing, but his eyes were narrow slits.

Martin's mom reached for a cookbook.

"I think I'll bake cookies," she said. "We can take some over to Alice's family when they get home. What kind should I make?"

"Chocolate chip," said Martin suspiciously. He knew she was trying to

distract him. But still, he loved cookies, and chocolate chip were his favorite.

"All right," she said. "Chocolate chip it is."

Martin took a deep breath to get back on track. The last time he had had his Faster Blaster was when he played Park Rangers at Alex's. But he was sure he had brought it home after that. If his mom had cleaned everywhere, then there was only one place left to look.

Martin headed outside to his tree house. He climbed up the ladder and through the hatch door. Then he searched every corner. Empty juice glasses. Stacks of *Zip Rideout* comics. A butterfly net. Dad's hammer.

Oops, thought Martin. His dad had been looking for that for days.

Martin looked around one last time, just to be sure.

Well. That was it. He had looked absolutely everywhere. It meant he had been right all along. Martin's ears began to burn.

Martin clambered back down and stormed across the lawn. He flung the kitchen door open. His mom was at the counter pouring chocolate chips into the cookie batter.

"Mom!" he yelled.

"Martin! You scared me!" she gasped, whirling around.

"You threw out my Faster Blaster!" accused Martin.

"I did what?"

"You threw out my Faster Blaster! I
know you did!" said Martin, finger pointing.

"Martin, I haven't seen —"

But Martin didn't wait to hear. He rifled
through the bags at the kitchen door one
by one, certain of what he would find. His

mom watched, arms crossed, as Martin searched the last bag.

But no Faster Blaster.

Martin stood up, confused and empty-handed. All he could do was run upstairs and fling himself onto his bed. But there was no escape.

"Are you going to tell me what's going on?" his mom demanded from his bedroom doorway when she caught up.

Martin curled to face the wall. He knew she wasn't going to go away, so at last he spoke.

"I just thought, well, the whole thing with Ginny, and then my missing blaster ..." His voice trailed off.

"You thought I was lying?" Her voice softened.

Martin nodded. She sat down with him and rubbed his back.

"I already told you. I wouldn't lie to you."

"Then what about Alice?"

"We went along with her parents' wishes and bought Alice a new hamster. But if you feel you must tell Alice about Ginny, then I think you should."

"Really?" he asked, rolling over.

"Really."

"Tell the truth?" he asked, sitting up.

"Yes, if you think that's the right thing to do."

Martin let this sink in for a moment. And then he remembered his own loss.

"So you really haven't seen my Zip Rideout H$_2$O Faster Blaster?" he asked one last time.

His mom sighed. "No, Martin. I really haven't." She gave him a hug, and he believed her.

"Now come downstairs. Help me bake some cookies for Alice."

Martin nodded and followed her to the kitchen. Later he got to lick the beaters while his mom arranged warm cookies on a plate. Then they headed over to Alice's house and rang the bell. Martin's heart began to pound as he thought about what he was going to say.

Alice opened the door, clutching an upside-down doll.

Martin took a step back. He had forgotten how little she was, and it rattled him.

"Hi, Martin! Mmm! Cookies!"

"Come on in," called Alice's mom as she came toward the door.

"Cookies, Mommy," said Alice. She

stared at the plate with big eyes.

"How lovely," said Alice's mom. She turned to Martin, who now stood half hidden behind his mom.

"Thank-you so much for taking care of Ginny."

"You ... you're welcome," Martin stammered. He shuffled his feet and glanced at Alice.

"Why don't you two take the cookies to the picnic table out back?" Alice's mom suggested.

"Goody!" cheered Alice, jumping up and down. Before Martin could say anything further, she grabbed his hand and led the way. They sat in the shade and munched on the still-warm cookies.

Martin prepared himself again. He'd start

off with some small talk. Ease into the truth.

"Are you ... glad to be home?" he asked
between bites.

"Yes. I missed Ginny. She's my best
friend in the whole world."

Cripes. Martin set down his half-eaten
cookie. He was no longer sure what to say.

Alice reached for another cookie, but stopped midway. She studied Martin's face.

"Are you sad?" she asked.

"No. Yes," said Martin, shifting on the bench.

Alice looked up at him with her springy little-girl pigtails and crooked pink barrettes.

"I'll miss taking care of Ginny," he said at last with a whoosh. Even as the words came out, he knew they were the right ones to say.

Alice nodded and patted his hand. "Hey, what's that?" she asked as she jumped up. She ran over to a little tree-shaded mound that was covered by freshly cut flowers.

"Those are for Ginny," Martin blurted before he caught himself.

"For Ginny!" Alice gushed with excitement as she bunched up the flowers. She ran inside with the bouquet.

Martin sat alone at the picnic table. After a moment, he smiled. Everything had worked out. He finished his cookie and waved at his mom in the window. Then he headed for home.

When he saw that his dad was vacuuming the van, Martin stopped to watch.

"Did everything go okay with Alice?" his dad asked over the noise.

"Yes," said Martin. "And she really liked the flowers you left for Ginny."

His dad nodded and turned off the vacuum.

"Hey! What do we have here?" His dad pulled out something wedged behind the seat cushion. A Zip Rideout H_2O Faster Blaster. He gave Martin a friendly squirt. Martin grinned.

His dad poured some soap into a bucket and filled it with water.

"Need some help?" asked Martin happily.

"That'd be great!" His dad put an arm around Martin, and they stood together taking in the cheerful welcome of spring peepers.

Martin thought about the beautiful spot his dad had picked out for Ginny in Alice's backyard. He thought about his mom's plate of homemade chocolate chip cookies. And he thought about the look-alike hamster he had found at  the pet store that needed a good home.

"I'm sorry about Ginny," Martin's dad said softly. "But you did a very kind thing today." He squeezed Martin's shoulder.

"We all did," said Martin. He dipped a rag into the soapy water and started to wash.

Smithereens

Martin loved Mondays because right after dinner he went to Junior Badgers. Each week his troop did something different. Tonight they were building model rockets.

Martin glued on the fins, working ever so carefully. It reminded him of his favorite television hero, Zip Rideout: Space Cadet. Zip was always fixing his rocket.

"Holy cow," said Alex, who had come over to see what Martin was up to. "Your fins are perfect!"

"Thanks," said Martin, shrugging modestly. He was used to nice comments about his artwork, and Alex was right. His fins *were* perfect.

Alex held up his own rocket. "What do you think?" he asked.

Cripes. As usual, Alex had not taken his time. Big gobs of glue oozed from his rocket fins, which were crooked. And it

looked like his rocket had crash-landed into a can of gray paint. Even his Badger shirt was splattered.

Martin was trying to think of something kind to say when Stuart joined them. He saw Alex's rocket and burst out laughing. "Ka-boom!" he said, throwing up his arms.

Alex ignored him. "What should I do, Martin?" he asked hopefully.

Martin studied the rocket. Whenever he glanced up, Stuart mouthed "ka-boom." Then Alex whipped around and saw what Stuart was doing. A shoving match started between the two, but Martin stepped in with an idea.

"How about painting flames on your rocket?" he suggested quickly.

"Good idea," said Alex, who shoved Stuart one last time before they both returned to their places.

Martin sighed. He wondered what Zip Rideout would do if he had two best friends who sometimes didn't get along. But Zip always fought evil alone.

"Oooh!"

"Aaah!"

Some Badgers had gathered around Alex. He held up his rocket so they could have a better look.

"Flames!" the crowd murmured.

Martin looked over. Wow! Flames beat plain rockets any day. He dipped his paintbrush in red and got to work.

"So you're copying Alex?" said Stuart, who had sauntered over for another visit.

"What do you mean?" asked Martin. "I'm the one who thought of the flames."

"Sure," said Stuart. "But Alex painted them first."

Martin sucked in his breath. He was about to argue when his thoughts were interrupted.

"Okay, Badgers!" announced Head Badger Bob. "Start packing up. You can finish your rockets at home. We'll launch them this Saturday at Tupper Grove Park!"

The troop cheered, and there was a flurry of activity as everyone tidied up.

Not Martin. He stood for a moment trying to shrug off Stuart's words. The flames *were* his idea, and they *did* look good, but he decided he would think of something else. Besides, there was plenty of time before Saturday's launch. He quickly painted over his flames and then headed to the door where his dad was waiting.

"Hi, Sport."

Before Martin could answer, Alex rushed by.

"Whoa!" said Martin's dad. "Nice flames, Alex. Well done!"

"Thanks, Mr. Bridge," said Alex, and he stopped to give Martin's dad a better look.

Martin's dad never said "well done" unless he really meant it. Martin looked at his own plain rocket and frowned.

"The flames were a good idea, weren't
they, Alex?" said Martin. He thought that
now would be a good time for Alex to
thank him, but Martin's dad cut in.

"Say, why don't you boys get together
this week to finish your rockets? We have
plenty of paint and brushes, right, Martin?"

"Sure," said Martin in a flat voice.

"How about Thursday?" asked Alex eagerly.

Martin nodded.

"Well. Gotta go," said Alex. He bolted for the coatrack.

"The flames were my idea," blurted Martin, but his dad didn't hear. He was asking Head Badger Bob about helping out at Saturday's launch.

Martin swallowed hard. A niggling feeling in his stomach told him that maybe he shouldn't have been so quick to give away his flames idea.

On Tuesday morning, Martin woke up with that same niggling feeling. It grew bigger each time Alex bragged about his rocket at school that day. Several times Martin was tempted to tell everyone that the flames were his idea, but Stuart's words burned in his head. So he fumed and said nothing.

When Martin got home from school, he flopped down on the sofa to watch his favorite cartoon.

"Let me guess, *Zip Rideout?*" his mom teased.

"Uh-huh," said Martin without taking his eyes off the action. "This is the one where Zip races his rocket in the Outer Space Olympics."

The competition was on. There were rockets with stripes. There were rockets with swirls. Some had polka dots. Some had checks. But there was only one with flames.

Zip Rideout's.

And Zip won gold.

"Arrgh!" said Martin as he clicked off the show. He was angry that he'd given away such a great idea. He was angry that Alex hadn't thanked him. And he still didn't know how to finish his own rocket.

By Wednesday
at dinner, Martin could
barely taste his food. It had been
another day of Alex gloating about the
flames. Another day of Alex not thanking
Martin. And another day of Martin staring
at his own unfinished rocket.

"You must be getting excited about
Saturday's big launch," said his dad between
bites. "How's your rocket coming along?"

"Lousy. I can't think of how to finish
it," said Martin glumly, pushing his mashed
potatoes around his plate.

They ate in silence.

"Say, I have an idea," said his mom.

She jumped up from the table, opened
a cupboard and plunked a box of cereal in
front of Martin. Zip Rideout Space Flakes.
On the back was a picture of Zip's rocket
painted with flames and blasting across
the sky.

"Flames!" said his mom, pointing to the
picture.

Martin barely glanced up.

"Can't," he said bitterly. "Flames are already ... taken." He almost spat out the words.

"Taken?" said his mom. "Oh. Well, I don't know what could be better than flames."

"Me, neither," muttered Martin. He scuffed at the floor.

"You'll think of something," she said brightly, the way mothers do when things look bad.

Martin didn't answer. He wouldn't have to think of something if it weren't for Alex taking his idea with not so much as a thank-you.

Wait a minute.

Alex hadn't thanked him because he

had stolen Martin's idea. That's right! *Stolen!* No wonder Martin felt rotten. He'd been robbed! His stomach churned as he pushed his plate away.

By Thursday, talk of Alex's rocket had spread far and wide. He never grew tired of chatting to anyone within lift-off range. Martin huffed and glared, but Alex didn't notice.

"Hey, Martin," Alex called when Martin tried to hide in the lineup for his bus home. "I'm coming over to your house tonight so we can finish our rockets. Remember?"

"Humph," said Martin over his shoulder. He took a step up onto the bus.

"See you after dinner then," said Alex without missing a beat.

Martin turned back and tried to think of a quick excuse, but Alex had already walked away. The bus door slapped shut. Martin had only one hope as he took his seat beside Stuart. Maybe Alex would forget to show up.

When the doorbell rang right after dinner, Martin's heart sank.

"What do you have there?" asked Martin's mom as she opened the door.

"My rocket," said the rocket expert. He held out the box that had been tucked under his arm.

"Oh, let's see!" she said, clapping her hands.

Alex lifted the lid and dramatically peeled away layer after layer of tissue paper. Martin wanted to snatch off the final layers and get on with it. He tapped his foot instead.

Finally Alex uncovered the rocket like a scientist showing off a new discovery. "Ta da!"

"It's gorgeous, Alex!" said Martin's mom. "Look, Martin! Flames!"

Martin glared at her. He now understood
why Zip Rideout's mom never appeared in
any of his shows.

"Can we get going already?" Martin
demanded with a scowl.

Without waiting
for an answer, he
shoved past Alex and
stomped upstairs to
his room. He yanked
open drawers and
rifled through his art
supplies.

Alex caught up
and stood in the
doorway. "What's
wrong with you?" he asked.

Martin stopped rifling. He wheeled
around to face Alex, anger exploding
inside him.

"What's wrong with me?! It's about
time you asked! But I guess you've been
too busy stealing my idea!"

"What idea?" asked Alex. His eyebrows shot up.

"Flames," said Martin, his ears burning. "The flames were my idea and you stole it!"

"I didn't steal anything!" said Alex. Now he scowled. "You gave me that idea, remember? You said I should paint flames. So I did."

Martin blinked hard.

Sensing victory, Alex picked up Martin's rocket and continued. "Paint flames, too. I don't care."

Martin snatched his rocket back. "I can't paint flames. Everyone will think *I* copied *you*!"

"Oh, I get it. You think you're too good to copy me."

That stopped Martin. He really *did* think he was too good to copy Alex.

"I thought so," said Alex smugly. "Well, if you're so good, why don't you think of a better idea than stupid old flames?"

"If they're so stupid," sputtered Martin, "why'd you steal them?"

Alex gave Martin a level glare.

"*Nobody* calls me a stealer," said Alex.

His words
dropped out like
ice cubes. He
stuffed his rocket
into its box and
piled the tissue
paper back in.
Without another
word, Alex
shut the lid
and stomped

downstairs to call his dad for a ride home.

"What's going on?" Martin's mom
demanded after Alex left.

"Alex stole my idea," declared Martin
hotly. He sat cross-armed on his bed.

"He did, did he?" she asked gently as
she sat down. "Was it the flames?"

Martin nodded miserably.

"That was a good idea," she said, patting his knee.

"Well, I know that now!" said Martin impatiently. "You should see all the to-do Alex has been getting."

"Good ideas do get a lot of attention," she agreed.

"But Alex didn't even thank me," he implored.

"Perhaps Alex forgot because he's not used to all the fuss."

Martin rolled his eyes.

"So what will you do about it now?"

"I'll show him! I'll think of something way better than flames."

"Oh, Martin," she said, shaking her head. "Revenge never works."

Revenge works for Zip Rideout, thought Martin, but he didn't say it out loud. He knew his mom would launch into a big talk if he did, and he was in no mood to hear any of it.

Instead he curled up tight and turned on his side to face the wall. His mom bent to give him a kiss, then left him alone with his thoughts.

When Martin woke up Friday morning, the first thing he saw was his unfinished rocket lying on his night table. It mocked him. Then he remembered his fight with Alex. His stomach churned.

"I don't feel so good," he announced at breakfast. "I think I should stay home."

"Oh. That's too bad," said his mom, feeling Martin's forehead. "You'll miss art class today."

Martin's heart did a leap. Art class was his favorite. Maybe there he would come up with an idea to finish his rocket in time for tomorrow's launch.

"I'm feeling a bit better," he said after polishing off a large bowl of Zip Rideout Space Flakes.

When Martin arrived at school, a crowd had gathered around the display case in the art room. Each week their teacher selected someone's work for the case. Martin's work had been chosen many times. Just last week he had painted a brilliant picture

of Zip Rideout. Martin smiled, sure that Zip
was this week's pick.

Martin squeezed past everyone to
admire his work in the display case.

No!

It couldn't be!

But there it was.

Flames and all.

Martin shoved his way back through the crowd and stormed over to a workspace in the farthest corner of the room. Alex proudly opened the case and gave a talk about his rocket, but Martin couldn't stand to hear one more word.

Instead he mixed colors furiously and began to paint a picture of a rocket exploding in space. It had flames just like Alex's. But Martin found it hard to concentrate with Alex yammering on and on, so the more paint he added the worse his picture got.

"Ka-boom!" called Stuart from across

the room. The crowd surrounding Alex
turned and saw the worst picture Martin
had painted since kindergarten. There
were gasps.

Martin stared back, red-faced. Zip
Rideout didn't need best friends. Neither
did he. His hands shook as he doubled the
wet painting over on itself. Then he folded
and folded until he had a tight square wad
that was as hard as the knot in his stomach.

When no one was looking, he pitched it at Alex's rocket.

But by now Alex's rocket had a force field all its own. Martin missed by a long shot. He knew then that Alex's rocket was unstoppable, and that Alex was sure to have a spectacular first flight at tomorrow's launch. Martin carried that dark thought for the rest of the day.

After school, Martin hugged his knees as he watched a *Zip Rideout* rerun. Zip had crash-landed on an unknown moon and was building jet packs for his rocket.

Martin bolted upright. Jet packs. That was it! Jet packs beat flames any day!

Martin rushed to his room. Building the jet packs was easy, and he used duct tape to fasten them on. When he stood back to

admire his work, the jet packs looked even
better than he expected. Zip Rideout would
be proud.

"Take that, Alex!" he said with
satisfaction.

Later Martin's dad came up to tuck him into bed. "You've finished your rocket," he said when he spotted it on Martin's night table. It stood poised ready for takeoff.

"Like the jet packs?" asked Martin, getting up on one elbow to have another look.

"They're a blast," said his dad, flicking off the lights.

Martin fell asleep smiling, his rocket glowing beside him in the moonlight.

Saturday morning. Launch day! Martin

was too excited to finish his bowl of Zip Rideout Space Flakes.

"Let's go! Let's go!" he insisted while his dad gulped down his coffee.

The drive took forever, but when Martin stepped onto the launch field at Tupper Grove Park, his rocket was an instant success.

"Jet packs," the Badgers murmured, nodding approval. Martin shrugged modestly.

Alex pushed through the crowd. Martin gave him a smug grin and held up his rocket so Alex could have a good, long look.

"I thought of jet packs *myself*," Martin announced. Alex's face fell. He turned away and lowered his rocket to his side as if it were a broken toy.

All of a sudden, Martin's pride whooshed out of him, like the time Zip

Rideout's parachute shot out of Zip's backpack but got tangled as he plummeted toward the ground. Zip had pulled a second emergency parachute and it filled, but Martin wasn't so lucky. He landed hard.

"Attention, Badgers!"

Everyone bumped past Martin and Alex to surround the launchpad. Rocket launchings beat jet packs any day.

"We're going to use extra-big fuel cells," announced Head Badger Bob, "so we can blast these rockets all the way to the moon!"

The troop buzzed with excitement, but Martin no longer cared about the launch. He glanced at Alex and tried to think of something kind to say.

"You ... did a great paint job with the flames," Martin tested in his warmest voice.

Alex wheeled around.

"Flames?" he snapped back. "You mean the flames you said I *stole*?"

A few Badgers turned their way. Fights beat rocket launchings any day.

"Boys, boys!" called Head Badger Bob. "We're ready for the first rocket. Do I have a volunteer?"

"Me!" called Alex, shooting Martin an icy glare. The troop cheered as he raced up and placed his rocket on the launchpad. His moment in the spotlight was back.

"All systems ready?"

"Roger," said Alex proudly.

Everyone stood back in a semicircle and began the countdown.

"Ten, nine, eight ..."

Martin was shaking.

"... seven, six, five ..."

Someone had tried to steal from a friend.

"... four, three, two ..."

But it wasn't Alex.

"... one ..."

It was me, Martin realized with a thud.

"Blast off!"

Alex's rocket flew, not up, but into a zillion pieces. The explosion forced the entire troop to run screaming for cover.

"Holy cow," said Alex in a small voice as bits of his rocket fell from the sky.

Martin stood up slowly along with the others, his ears burning. He remembered his spiteful painting of Alex's rocket and hoped no one else did. Especially Alex.

"Maybe your fuel cells are too big for these rockets," Martin's dad called over.

"Could be," said Head Badger Bob, dusting off his pants. "Or maybe that was just a bad fuel cell. Let's try one more rocket." He smiled the way leaders do when they aren't so sure. "Do I have a volunteer?"

The entire troop shuffled a step back. Each Badger clutched his prized rocket and

looked away. Like the rest of the troop, Martin was certain the next rocket would be blown to smithereens, too.

Still, he wondered if Zip Rideout had ever felt as lonely as he did now.

"Try mine," he called.

"Are you sure, Sport?" whispered Martin's dad.

"It's just a rocket," Martin said in his bravest voice. He stepped forward and placed it on the launchpad.

"Stand back!" announced Head Badger Bob.

"Way back!" shouted Martin's dad.

The troop started the countdown, but many of the Badgers didn't wait. They had already hit the ground with their hands over their heads.

"Blast off!" shouted the ones still standing.

Martin's rocket exploded just like Alex's, jet packs and all.

The Badgers slowly got to their feet. Dazed, Head Badger Bob scratched his head.

He stared at the charred smudges on the launchpad that had once been two splendid rockets.

"I'd say that's enough for today," said Martin's dad in a firm voice. He patted Martin on the back before marching over to Head Badger Bob for a few words.

The troop cheered and broke into a game of tag. Alex did not join in. He sat down by the launchpad. Martin sat beside him. For a while they plucked at the grass and said nothing. At last Martin spoke.

"I guess extra-big fuel cells beat jet packs and flames any day." He was beginning to think the whole thing a bit funny. There was more silence and then ...

"Ka-boom!" shouted Alex, throwing up his arms like Stuart.

They turned to each other and burst
out laughing.

"Say, Martin," said Alex when he
recovered. "Maybe you could paint a
picture of our rockets. You know, before
they blew up and everything."

"Great idea," said Martin, giving Alex
a playful punch on the shoulder.

Martin could already see what he would
paint. Two glorious rockets soaring side by

side into an unknown galaxy. One would have flames. The other would have jet packs. And his picture would be so good, he just knew it would be chosen for the display case.

Martin sprang to his feet, then pulled Alex up with the strength of ten superheroes.

"Let's join the troop!" Alex said, and he punched Martin back.

Together they crossed the field, stepping over exploded bits and pieces without having to say another word.

Zip Rideout would be jealous. Sure, he knew how to fix rockets. But Martin had figured out how to fix friendship.

And friendship beats rockets any day.